DC COMICS SUPER HEROES

CARNIVAL CAPERS!

STORY BY ERIC M. ESQUIVEL
ILLUSTRATED BY SEAN WANG

SCHOLASTIC

SCHOLASTIC CHILDREN'S BOOKS
EUSTON HOUSE,
24 EVERSHOLT STREET,
LONDON NWI IDB, UK

A DIVISION OF SCHOLASTIC LTD
LONDON ~ NEW YORK ~ TORONTO ~ SYDNEY ~ AUCKLAND
MEXICO CITY ~ NEW DELHI ~ HONG KONG

THIS BOOK WAS FIRST PUBLISHED IN THE US IN 2016 BY SCHOLASTIC INC.
PUBLISHED IN THE UK BY SCHOLASTIC LTD, 2016

ISBN 978 1407 16434 2

PRINTED AND BOUND IN MALAYSIA

2 4 6 8 10 9 7 5 3 1

PAPERS USED BY SCHOLASTIC CHILDREN'S BOOKS ARE MADE FROM WOODS
GROWN IN SUSTAINABLE FORESTS.

WWW.SCHOLASTIC.CO.UK

BENEATH WAYNE MANOR LIES THE BATCAVE,
SECRET HQ TO BATMAN AND ROBIN!

OH NO! WHAT COULD THAT SOUND BE? IS THE DYNAMIC DUO IN TROUBLE?

NOT QUITE. BEAST BOY AND STARFIRE ARE FIGHTING OVER WHO GETS TO ADD ICING TO THEIR CAKE.

SUPER HERO TRAINING 101: HOME EC

"I WANT TO ADD THE ICING, STARFIRE!" BEAST BOY SAYS.

"AW, MAN! I WANTED TO ADD THE ICING!" ROBIN SAYS.

"YOU CAN'T <u>ALL</u> BE ON ICING DUTY," BATMAN SAYS. "YOU HAVE TO PRACTISE WORKING TOGETHER AS A TEAM! TEAMWORK IS <u>MORE POWERFUL</u> THAN ANY GIZMO IN YOUR UTILITY BELT."

ALFRED HAS AN IDEA! "PERHAPS A BREAK IS IN ORDER?" HE ASKS. "MAYBE ROBIN AND HIS FRIENDS COULD FIND OUT ABOUT THAT STRANGE NEW CARNIVAL IN TOWN?"

WHILE WALKING ALONE THROUGH THE CARNIVAL, STARFIRE STOPS BY A STRANGE-LOOKING RIDE.

"YOU THINK YOU'RE TOUGH ENOUGH TO RIDE THE FLOWER TOWER, LITTLE GIRL?" THE CARNIVAL WORKER ASKS.

ROBIN IS WALKING BY A DUNK TANK.
"TRY YOUR LUCK?" THE CARNIVAL WORKER ASKS.
"SURE!" ROBIN SAYS. "GET READY — I'VE GOT
PRETTY GOOD AIM."

IT'S A TRAP! THOSE AREN'T CARNIVAL WORKERS, THEY'RE SUPER-VILLAINS!
"NOW THAT WE'VE GOT YOU, WE CAN RIDE ALL THE RIDES WE WANT," THE JOKER SAYS.

BATMAN HAS A LOT OF FRIENDS HE CAN CALL ON WHEN HE NEEDS HELP! THEY'RE A GREAT TEAM.

EVEN SUPER HEROES CALL ON FRIENDS WHEN THEY'RE IN NEED OF HELP!

THE SUPER-VILLAINS ALL SPLIT UP BUT THE GOOD GUYS WORK TOGETHER AS A TEAM!

"SORRY, BLACK MANTA, BUT THERE'S NO CANDY FLOSS IN JAIL," NIGHTWING SAYS.

HA! HA! HA!

AQUAMAN AND THE FLASH PUT
THE BRAKES ON HARLEY QUINN . . .

FINALLY, THE JOKER'S SEEING GREEN WHEN HAWKMAN AND GREEN LANTERN STOP HIS STEAMROLLER IN ITS TRACKS.

THE SUPER-VILLAINS ARE ALL TIED UP!